RAGTIME TUMPIE

WRITTEN BY
ALAN SCHROEDER

PAINTINGS BY
BERNIE FUCHS

LITTLE, BROWN AND COMPANY

New York · An AOL Time Warner Company

Ragtime Tumpie is a fictional account of the childhood of the entertainer Josephine Baker. While some scenes have been invented, the basic facts are true.

For further reading, Lynn Haney's *Naked at the Feast* (Dodd, Mead & Company, 1981) is a spirited biography of Josephine's life and times. Unfortunately out of print, Haney's book contains much of the background information that appears in *Ragtime Tumpie*.

To my family . . .

and also to Rick

A.S.

Text copyright © 1989 by Alan Schroeder
Illustrations copyright © 1989 by Bernie Fuchs

First Paperback Edition

Library of Congress Cataloging-in-Publication Data

Schroeder, Alan.
Ragtime Tumpie/by Alan Schroeder; illustrated by Bernie Fuchs.
— 1st ed.
    p.   cm.
Summary: Tumpie, a young black girl who will later become famous as the dancer Josephine Baker, longs to find the opportunity to dance amid the poverty and vivacious street life of St. Louis in the early 1900s.
ISBN 0-316-77497-9 (hc)
ISBN 0-316-77504-5 (pb)
    1. Baker, Josephine, 1906–1975 — Juvenile fiction. [1. Baker, Josephine, 1906–1975 — Fiction. 2. Afro-Americans — Fiction. 3. Dancing — Fiction. 4. Saint Louis (Mo.) — Fiction.] I. Fuchs, Bernie, ill. II. Title.
PZ7.S3796Rag   1989
[E] – dc19   87-37221

10 9 8

SC

Manufactured in China.

Each morning, before the sun was up, Tumpie walked two miles to the Soulard Market. The Market was a big old place, full of carrots and tomatoes and soggy wooden lettuce crates. There, she hid under the farmers' stalls and snatched up the vegetables and fruits that fell on the ground.

"I see you, Tumpie!" the farmers laughed, and Tumpie grinned.

Then, putting the apples and tomatoes into her little wagon, she'd start home, back to Gratiot Street, the poorest section of St. Louis.

This morning, as she passed the Rosebud Café on Market Street, the tinny sounds of a pianola spilled out onto the sidewalk, and inside, Tumpie could hear a red-hot mama singing "Wild Cherries."

It was the summer of 1915, and St. Louis was jumping. Music was everywhere. Ragtime music.

Tumpie dropped the wagon handle and leaned up against the café wall. Standing there in the sunlight, she listened to the strumming of the banjos, to the high-pitched cry of the clarinet, and to the tinkling of the keys as the piano man ran his fingers up the scale. The catchy rhythm jumped to her toes and her foot began tapping out the beat on the pavement.

Ragtime was piano music, happy music, and it always made Tumpie think of Eddie, her honky-tonk daddy. Eddie didn't live with them anymore. He'd moved out a long time ago, and Tumpie's stepfather had moved in. Tumpie knew her daddy wasn't coming back, but she still liked to remember all the fun they used to have, back when Eddie would whip out his sticks and set up his drums anywhere — picnics and barrel houses, riverboats and gambling halls.

At night, Tumpie's mama would take her to the honky-tonks to hear Eddie and his friends play. Everyone had loved watching Eddie, especially when he'd lean back, close his eyes, and lick the snare drum with the tips of his sticks. Then the place would really heat up.

"Dill Pickles Rag."

"Frog Legs Rag."

"Chicken Chowder."

The catchiest music in the nation, and Tumpie had heard it all.

In the afternoons, Eddie would stand in front of the pool halls, strutting and showing off his shiny new shoes. He carried his drumsticks everywhere, and sometimes, when he wasn't throwing dice, he'd bend down and beat the sticks on the cracked cement.

"Hear that, honey?" he'd say to Tumpie. "That's called syncopation!"

"Syn-co-pa-tion!" Tumpie would shout, and she'd skip out the beat on the sidewalk.

Then Eddie would show her a two-step he'd learned at the Dance Academy, tossing his sticks high into the air, where they'd spin like fire against the sun. The two of them would start clapping and laughing, and on days like that, the whole street seemed alive with dancing and color and the fast joy of ragtime music.

Tumpie was still lost in thought when the train whistle blew. She jumped and started pulling her wagon. She knew she'd better get down to the tracks. Once a week, her stepfather, Arthur, sent her down to Union Station to pick up the coal that had fallen off the hopper cars. She didn't mind, though. The coal kept them warm at night, and besides, she liked watching the trains. The trains went everywhere.

A block away, Tumpie could hear the Knickerbocker pulling in from New York, and as she got closer to the tracks, she began thinking of all the places she'd like to see, like the dance halls in Harlem, where the girls wore fancy dresses and the jazz men played till dawn.

"I wish I could get on a train and just ride away," she thought, picking up the black, dusty lumps.

As soon as the wagon was loaded up, coal on one end, fruits and vegetables on the other, Tumpie headed for home. Rounding the corner, she caught her reflection in the window of the Four Deuces Saloon. She smiled at it. Then she crossed her eyes and made a face. Someone inside started laughing, and that made her laugh, too. So, doing her daddy's two-step, she kicked out her legs and pretended she was a world-famous honky-tonker.

"I'm Ragtime Tumpie!" she laughed, and as she skipped down the sidewalk, the apples and tomatoes bounced up and down in her wagon.

By the time she got home, one of the wheels was loose and the bananas were brown from the sun. As she let herself into the apartment, Tumpie could hear her mama and stepfather talking. Carrie's voice sounded heavy and tired, and Arthur was complaining.

"I'm home," Tumpie called, taking the bruised fruit out of the wagon and putting it on the kitchen table.

"You're late," Arthur said. "What happened?"

"Nothin'." Tumpie pushed the wagon into its corner. "Got some apricots. Real sweet, too."

Arthur grunted. "What were you doin'?" he said. "Dancing in the street again? Makin' a fool of yourself?"

Tumpie looked Arthur right in the eye, apricot juice dripping down her chin.

"I'm gonna be a honky-tonk dancer," she told him, "and I'm gonna make lots of money!"

"Oh, sure," he said. "And I'm gonna be President!"

He laughed and walked out the door.

The air that night was hot and muggy. In bed, Tumpie could hear the distant sounds of pianos and laughter, and women singing the blues in the dark: "My man done gone away. Now the blues done hit me hard . . ."

She thought of her daddy, and the barrel house banjos and the fast rags, and the hot, red lights of Chestnut Valley. Down the street, she could hear the band playing "Cotton Bolls," real slow and sad-like. She closed her eyes, and little by little, the lazy, bluesy sound of the saxophones lulled Tumpie to sleep.

The months passed. Winter came early, and the snow hung thick on the windowsills. In December, the apartment was so cold that Tumpie danced just to keep warm.

"Kick those legs up," Carrie told her, "and clap your hands. If you gonna dance, girl, you gotta have rhythm!"

Sometimes, Carrie would put down her broom and the two of them would dance together, and Tumpie would pretend they were on the stage of the Booker T. Washington Theater and that she was the star. The apartment seemed less cold then, and even Arthur stopped being such an old sourpuss.

When spring came, she kept dancing. Once a week, the neighborhood kids put on a vaudeville show, and Tumpie got to dance in the chorus. The seats were made out of orange crates and the curtain was nothing but a handful of rags, but Tumpie did the bunny hug until beads of sweat ran down her forehead and the planks of the wooden stage rattled.

"You're gonna wear out your feet, girl!" her mama told her.

But Tumpie didn't care. All summer long she danced barefoot up and down the hot St. Louis sidewalks.

Then, one morning, Medicine Man came to town. His rickety wagon was filled with colorful bottles.

"Step right up!" he said. "My potions can cure anything!"

The people in the neighborhood began to gather around.

Medicine Man stayed all day.

He sold snake oil and rheumatism tonic, and ancient powders "stolen from the Great Pyramids of Egypt."

He never stopped talking, and one by one, all of the colorful bottles were sold.

Then, darkness slowly fell. It was a hot, steamy St. Louis night. The kerosene torches were lit and someone started playing the harmonica.

Medicine Man grinned.

"We're gonna have a dancin' contest," he said.

A fiddler stepped forward. The harmonica man played faster, and everyone started clapping and stomping their feet.

Tumpie stood near the edge of the crowd and watched, her fingers drumming a fire hydrant. One by one, people climbed up onto the stage and danced to the ragtime music. Even old Savannah, heavy as she was, got up and threw her big hips around. Her bandana was a swirl of hot color.

"Can I go up?" Tumpie begged her mama.

"You're too little," Carrie whispered. "Anyway, it's time for your bed."

Just then, Medicine Man pulled something out of his hat.

"I got a shiny silver dollar for the winner," he promised.

Suddenly, Tumpie was pushing her way through the crowd.

"I ain't too little!" she cried. "Oh, please, mister, oh, please, let me dance. I ain't too little!"

Medicine Man laughed and pulled her up onto the stage. The clapping and the stomping seemed to get faster and louder.

"What's your name?" he asked.

"Tumpie," she said, staring at the silver dollar.

"Well, you go to it, sweet pea," and he pushed her to the center of the stage.

The air was sharp with the smell of kerosene. At the back of the crowd, Carrie watched as the harmonica man began counting out a beat. The fiddler caught the rhythm and swung his bow, music jumped from the little harmonica, and Tumpie, barefoot and burning with excitement, started to dance.

It was a fast rag, the kind her daddy used to heat up the honky-tonks with. Real jug band jazz. Tumpie closed her eyes, kicked out her legs, and pretended she was on the stage of the Booker T. Washington Theater. The crowd roared. She clapped her hands, threw her head back, and laughed and laughed.

Then, before she knew it, before she'd hardly started, the rag was over. But the crowd was still yelling, and Tumpie was still dancing.

She felt dizzy when Medicine Man handed her the silver dollar.

"No doubt about it, you won the contest!" he grinned.

The night sky echoed with the whoops and the cheers.

"Mama," Tumpie cried, "did you hear that, Mama? He said I won! I won!" She couldn't believe it. A silver dollar! For dancing!

Carrie hugged her tight. "You were real good, Tumpie, real good."

Tumpie could hardly stand still. "I'm gonna be a dancer, Mama, that's what I'm gonna be!"

"'Course you are, honey." Carrie took her by the hand. "Now, come on home. Why, look at you, you're all tired out."

"But, Mama —"

"Come on, Tumpie."

The crowd was breaking up. Next to the stage, someone started dousing the kerosene torches. Tumpie was still staring at the silver dollar in her hand. "I'll never stop dancin' now!"

Carrie smiled. "'Course not, sugar. Now, come on. Time for bed."

Across the street, Medicine Man had packed up his wares and was climbing into his wagon. He yawned as he took the reins in his hand.

"Giddyup," he said.

The wagon lurched forward.

As he passed by, Tumpie heard Medicine Man let out a deep sigh.

"Lord, it's been a long, long day, and heaven's still a mile away . . ."

Then the streets were empty and still. Blocks away, someone was singing the blues.

A cat meowed.

Tumpie slipped the silver dollar into her pocket, took Mama's hand, and the two of them set off for home.

Bettmann Archive

Author's Note

Tumpie never lost her love for dancing. When she grew up, she became a famous entertainer, the legendary Josephine Baker.

At the age of fourteen, with hardly a nickel to her name, Josephine joined the Dixie Steppers and left St. Louis to begin her career as a performer. After appearing in the Broadway show *Shuffle Along,* she sailed for Paris, where she tied a string of bananas around her waist and danced a wild Charleston. To the French, she was "le jazz hot," and she quickly became one of the most flamboyant and best-loved entertainers of her day.

Later, she starred in the *Ziegfeld Follies,* and in 1937 she became a French citizen. During World War II, she worked for the French Resistance and was awarded several medals for her bravery. In the 1950s, to promote world peace, Josephine Baker began adopting children of all nationalities. She called her family the "Rainbow Tribe."

She died in Paris in 1975.